Master Salt
the Sailors' Son

by ALLAN AHLBERG

with pictures by
ANDRÉ AMSTUTZ

PUFFIN

PUFFIN BOOKS
Published by the Penguin Group: London, New York, Australia,
Canada, India, Ireland, New Zealand and South Africa
Penguin Books Ltd, Registered Offices: 80 Strand, London WC2R 0RL, England

puffinbooks.com

First published by Viking 1980
Published in Puffin Books 1980
This edition published 2008
This edition produced for The Book People Ltd, Hall Wood Avenue,
Haydock, St Helens, WA11 9UL

2

Educational Advisory Editor: Brian Thompson

Made and printed in China

Mr Salt the sailor sailed the seven seas.
Mrs Salt sailed the seven seas as well.
So did Miss Salt.
Master Salt did not sail the seas.
He was too little.
He stayed on shore with his grandpa.

One day exciting things happened.
Mr and Mrs Salt got ready for a voyage.
"We are going to sail to
Coconut Island," they said.
Their ship was called the *Jolly Jack*.

Mr Salt cleaned the cabins
and washed the deck.
Mrs Salt and Sally Salt painted the funnel.
Sammy Salt sulked.
He wanted to go on a voyage too.

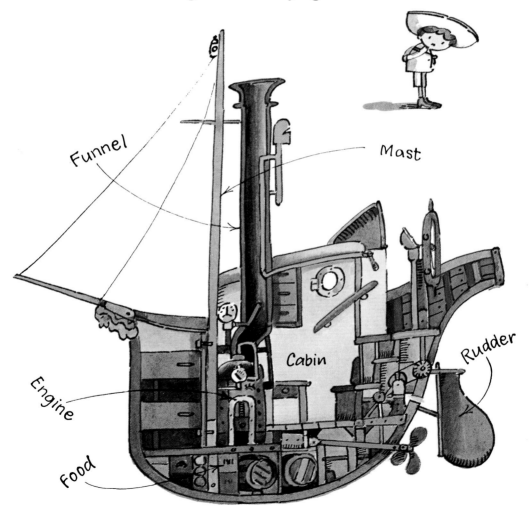

The next day the *Jolly Jack*
was ready to sail.
Mr and Mrs Salt pulled up the anchor.
Grandpa Salt stood on the shore.
But where was Sammy Salt?

The *Jolly Jack* sailed out to sea.
Sally Salt blew a kiss to her grandpa.
He waved goodbye from the shore.
But *where* was Sammy Salt?

The voyage began.
The *Jolly Jack* sailed past a lighthouse.
Sally Salt got the dinner ready.
Somebody's little hand reached out.
"Who's been eating *my* fish?" said Mr Salt.

The *Jolly Jack* sailed past
a big ship.

Mr Salt got the tea ready.
Somebody's little hand reached out again.
"Who's been eating *my* boiled egg?"
said Mrs Salt.

The *Jolly Jack* sailed past a whale.
Mrs Salt got the supper ready.
Somebody's little hand reached out again!
"Who's been drinking *my* cocoa?"
said Sally Salt.

In the night strange things happened.
Sally Salt woke up.
She said her nose kept tickling.
"Don't be silly, Sally," said Mr Salt.
Then Mr Salt went to bed and *he* woke up.
"My nose keeps tickling," he said.

In the morning more strange things happened.
Somebody's little footprints appeared on deck.
Somebody's little teeth-marks
appeared in an apple.
When Mr Salt was fishing,
somebody's little boot appeared
on the end of his line.

Then, in the afternoon,
terrible things happened.
There was a storm.
The rain fell and the wind blew.
The thunder thundered and
the lightning flashed.
The *Jolly Jack* tipped up and down
– and Mr Salt fell overboard!
"Man overboard!" shouted Mr Salt.

Mrs Salt came to the rescue.
But still the *Jolly Jack* tipped up
and down – and *she* fell overboard!
"Woman overboard!" shouted Mrs Salt.
Sally Salt came to the rescue.
But still the *Jolly Jack* tipped up
and down – and *she* fell overboard!
"Girl overboard!" shouted Sally Salt.

The next minute surprising things happened.
Somebody appeared on deck.
He threw a rope to Mr Salt.
"That's clever!" said Mr Salt.
He threw a lifebelt to Mrs Salt.
"Just what I need!" Mrs Salt said.
He threw a rubber-ring to Sally Salt.
She did not say a word.
He rescued them all!

"What a surprise!" said Mrs Salt.
"Look who it is!" said Mr Salt.
"It's Sammy!" said Sally.
Sammy Salt made hot drinks for
his family.
He wrapped them up in blankets.
He steered the ship.

It was me

"Now I know who tickled my nose,"
said Mr Salt.
"And drank my cocoa," said Sally Salt.
"And ate my boiled egg!" Mrs Salt said.
"That's right," said Sammy Salt. "It was me!"

After that the best things happened.
The storm blew away.
The *Jolly Jack* reached
Coconut Island.

There was a picnic on the shore,
and paddling in the sea,
and hide-and-seek in the jungle.

Bedtime came.
Mr and Mrs Salt and the children
slept out under the stars.
Then, in the night,
the last thing happened.
Sammy Salt woke up.
"My nose keeps tickling," he said.

The End